Voices from the Heart

Second Edition

William Power

TO PASTOR MANNY
& DAMIR

my DEAR family
in chRist

William Power

ISBN: 1477498729
ISBN-13: 978-1477498729

DEDICATION

To my mother Susan and Ashley Sue—I love you both—see you soon!

CONTENTS

Acknowledgments VIII

1 Dark Harvest Page 1

2 The Kiss of a Forbidden Lover Page 6

3 A Lesson in Love Page 9

4 The Tax Collector Page 13

5 What a Difference a Day Makes Page 18

6 Amends Page 21

7 The Country Store Page 24

8 To Find Wisdom Page 26

9 Leann Page 28

10 Wade Page 31

11 Love is in the little things Page 33

12 The Vase Page 35

13 Alone in the Night Page 37

14 A Night of Silent Rain Page 39

15 Want Page 40

16 My Adversary Page 41

17 I miss you Susan Dee   Page 43

18 I Fear The Night   Page 45

19 A New Love   Page 46

20 Memories of Spring   Page 47

21 A Christmas Past and Present Page 48

22 To a Friend   Page 50

23 Man`s Best Friend   Page 52

24 I`m stuck in here   Page 53

25 The Blue Ridge   Page 55

26 The Master Comes   Page 56

27 The Old Dusty Book   Page 58

28 Sadness   Page 59

29 The thorn in my side   Page 61

30 Escape From Wrath   Page 63

31 Love has blind eyes   Page 65

32 Death of a love   Page 67

33 The Bondage of Self   Page 69

34 Redemption   Page 70

35 The Cult of Personality   Page 71

36 You won, or did you?   Page 73

37 Ashley Sue   Page 74

38 The Wind   Page 76

    About the Author   Page 77

ACKNOWLEDGMENTS

There are so many people who have influenced my life greatly and helped me to arrive at my dream of publishing this book. First and foremost is Bill W. Without his testimonies in my life I would not be the man I am today. Secondly, I learned to find my voice as a writer from Anne Lamott and her book "Bird by Bird." She was so funny, real, down to earth, and sometimes neurotic in her book—I hope I can thank her personally someday. Finally, and absolutely, I want to acknowledge my Lord and Savior—Jesus Christ—without him nothing is possible. WP

1
Dark harvest

What do we do when life throws us a horrible curve ball and we lose either someone or something that we thought we could not live without? This is one of the most dreaded things we can face other than—possibly--the diagnosis of some fatal illness.

When the reality of what just happened to us finally kicks in, we are at first shocked, then dismayed, filled with fear—an identity crisis sometimes sets in—it`s really tough. The inability to see or understand the final outcome of these situations is a true dilemma that we face and live through in this life. It may be weeks, months, or years before we see the spiritual truths revealed through the pain we suffer in this world. Often times we find that in the end, the pain led to an important lesson, an important new direction, or to something worthwhile in life. That is the message in the story I am about to tell. The story is true and the events were real.

I knew a man who was in an organization for some years that was everything to him. He was a true blue believer in their philosophies and edicts. He would have given his life for their cause and at one point almost did. At the time he joined this group (who shall remain unnamed to protect the innocent) he was not a practicing Christian, he was saved yes, but was not living in Gods will by any stretch. He loved the comradeship and lifestyle of this group and he planned to remain a member until the day he died. He gave up most of the things that would be important to normal people to give his time and energy to this group. He put his family, his children, and his God on the back burner to be a loyal member.

During the course or his association with this group he changed. He became hard, he became someone he was not, and he went against all of the ethical boundaries he had once believed in. For many years his only goal was to be at the top, to be a leader in the organization, and to be a shot caller. He was willing to do or become whatever he must to achieve this goal.

The one reality in life that we all must face is that no matter what group you belong to, if there are people involved, there will be politics, neurotic behavior, jealousy, and deceit--It`s human nature in a fallen world. As a Christian, I have been hurt by Church members--at times--worse than the heathens I used to hang with. This is just life; there is no way around it.

Back to my story: As time went on he began to feel the weight of his sins and he knew he needed to change. At this time in his membership he had become a leader in the organization. He was an officer and he basically controlled about 150-200 members in 7 states. As in all groups, when you're a leader, there is a target on your back, you have enemies, you have political rivals, and his case was no different. There was a member of the group named Martin who was not well liked yet this man yearned to be a leader, he wanted recognition, he was hungry for power. Our man, we will call him Jake, was his friend and so Jake helped him begin to climb that ladder and share in his success as a regional officer.

Jake was a leader who worked closely (for many years) with the organizations top leadership. Jake had the clout and the ability to convince them that Martin was not who they thought he was. Jake defended him to the leadership and built him up every chance he had to put in a good word for him; eventually they listened and Martin was on his way. After a year or two he was even promoted to a higher office than Jake; Jake was proud of him, he deserved it, and Jake celebrated his victory.

Then it began to happen. In the years prior, Martin was at times very jealous of Jake`s personal success and clout within the group. He even conspired to have Jake thrown out of the organization at one point and damn near succeeded. Jake thought they had worked through all of those issues, especially given he had helped him in his ascent in the leadership hierarchy—he was wrong.

Over the next two years Martin did everything he could to discredit Jake, spread false rumors, and turn the leadership against him. Just like the Devil himself, Martin was a master manipulator of the truth. Satan never tells a lie that does not have a least a small bit of truth in it. His mastery is in telling just enough of the truth to make a lie become the truth. This man was just as crafty and wise in his trade. Having said that, the truth was that Jake was no Angel either; he had a past that was littered with violence and ego. At first Martin almost went too far too quickly and the leadership began to question him and his motive. He got smart and realized he should go after his goal one bite, one story, and one lie at a time. Martin realized he could not undermine Jake through the President; Jake was too close to this man, but that he would build his lies up through another important member of the leadership. He knew this member would convince the President that Martin was right. Months later at a called meeting—Jake would figure it all out; however, by then it was too late.

It was at this time that Jake finally turned to the Lord. Jake was due to meet the leadership the next weekend to straighten things out between himself and his rival officer .Jake had tried to make his case to the leadership, he had other members close to him give their stories as well. The other members saw it all, they knew how Martin was behaving when the leadership was not around—none of them knew that the President had turned and was now on Martin`s side. Jake had a bad gut feeling about the meeting. He was not sure why, but he felt he needed Gods help. He went to church for the first time in quite a while; he knelt at the church alter and gave it all to God.

When Jake arrived at the location of the meeting he soon noticed that all the other members and officers were treating him funny, something was different. Jake knew something was up but had no idea what the truth was. Soon, he saw the top officer of the organization— the President--a man he had shown undying loyalty to for over 14 years of his life. He knew that if this man, this officer, treated him in the normal fashion—if he greeted him in the normal way--that everything would turn out ok. The President met him with a hug and a smile.

Jake walked into the meeting. The meeting was held in a garage. The chairs were set in a circle and all the leadership and their security were circled around. Jake was not afraid, he had trained all these guys, he knew them personally, and he did not know what was about to take place. Jake took his normal posture--relaxed, confident the issues at hand would be resolved, and he waited for the President to speak. Jake had a gun in his front pocket. The security guys all knew this was his habit—to carry a 380 in his front pocket, but they never searched him or asked for his gun. He thought this was a good sign.

Jake knew that the leadership wanted to resolve the issues he had with his rival, but he had no clue that at this moment he had been completely undermined by him. The leadership did not trust Jake, they no longer cared about his service, his dedication, or any of the sacrifices he had made to the organization in the past—little did Jake know that he was seen as nothing less than an enemy to the organization.

The words that came out of the Presidents mouth rang in Jakes head for the next week, in his sleep, while he was awake, and they shocked him to his core…

"Jake…turn in your shit, you`re done, you`re out, you`re banished."

Jack felt his heart drop to his stomach. He sat frozen in time. The memories of 14 years flashed through his brain; the good times, the bad times, the night he was almost shot to death defending the patch he wore and the other men who died that night right in front of his eyes; the absolute loyalty and devotion he had for the man who had just thrown him to the curb. He slowly stood up, walked to the President, took off his cut, and walked out the door. The security escorted Jake to the gate and he left--broken, humiliated, and shocked.

He went back to the motel where he stayed to pack his bike for the long ride home. As he was packing he saw men posted around the hotel to make sure he left town and did not return to the camp to seek revenge. They all knew what Jake was capable of; however, they had no clue his heart had changed.

The ride home was grueling and bittersweet. His head ran back and forth between anger, revenge, and fear. His whole identity was now somehow in question—he had spent 14 years of his life with this organization, and now, it was all gone. What would he do? Who was he?

As Jake thought, he began to remember the prior weekend at church. He remembered that when he knelt down to pray he asked God to remove the anger, pain, and resentment from his life. He looked up at the sky and told God, "This was not what I meant," but in his heart he heard that still small voice saying to him: "Trust in me my son. I have good plans for your life. I only want your happiness and success. You could not be the man I want you to be while you were in this club."

Yes, Jake was in a motorcycle club. He had given his life and loyalty to this club for over 14 years. It was his family, it was his life, and the patch he wore was all that mattered to him. God removed him from a life of violence and pain. God showed Jake that his greatest pains, his greatest failure, his darkest past could be an asset to those he would help someday. All things work together for the good of those who love the Lord.

Jake went on to become college educated in his 40`s. He followed a dream of his from long before the club to become a writer. He found a new life, success, and today he lives a life devoted to God, his family, and peace. Jake at first began to reap the dark harvest he had sown all the many years before; however, God had a different plan when Jake finally called on his name.

2
THE KISS OF A FORBIDDEN LOVER

In some forms of art there are hidden stories, poetic songs, mystical meanings that one must figure out, or, they are simply a fantasy for the mind to wonder through. Paintings capture a moment in time, an act on the stage of humanity caught for a second, or display the imaginary moment in the creative mind of the artist. It was such a tale that this writer found in the painting of a man and woman embraced in a kiss.

The painting to some may seem boring or simple; however, behind this painting is the story of two lovers who were so passionate for one another their hearts could not hold still. They hungered for every minute they may spend together, the moments apart seemed as days or even century`s; their moments together disappeared in a flash as when lightning strikes the ground. In this painting there can be no doubt that these two lovers must hide their love for one another--an affair, a mistress, a heroic knight of whom the princess must not see.

They have been apart for quite some time as he was off to war. She was unable to confirm his true condition and was almost sure he was killed in battle. As reports came back to the castle she dared not ask of her lover`s fate lest someone know of their secret love. She waited and watched knowing that someone would surely mention his name--

someone would report the loss of such a great knight. She thought to herself surely this must mean he`s alive.

As the day loomed on she heard nothing of her lover`s fate. She walked to the tower above from which a better vantage point could be achieved; she felt no desire to go on living if her heroic prince did not return. She wept.

As she lay on the cold floor of the castle her heart weighed down in agonizing pain, she began to recite an old lover`s poem she had once heard long ago:

My Love is a Prison
I awoke from a nightmare filled with cold seat,
It seems I am destined to live in regret.
You control me by night no relief til` the day.
You stalk me, ghosts haunt me, I can`t get away

I reach for the past and I seek for what`s right.
I see only darkness, no child of the light.
I remember the good days but the pain is still real,
How much of my future will my past come and steal?

Please tell me my loved one who always remains;
How to forget you and let go the reigns;
How do I look back without the regret?
Will I be free, will I ever forget?

I shake in the night with a fever it seems;
Alone in my bed I`m controlled by the dreams,
I awake and I reach but my love is not there,
I swim in my sweat filled with pain and despair.

I lost you my love, seems a long time ago;
Please let me sleep, please let me let go.
I think in my mind that someday I`ll be free;
Then there you are in the shadows I see.

The mind is a terrible place to be chained,
The regrets of a life and a love that remain,
I miss you my love and I will until death;
I miss your warm kiss and the feel of your breath.

7

Someday I`ll die and until then ever be,
A prisoner of shadows, it`s you that I see;
Forgive me my love when I try to escape,
For a live without you I cannot contemplate

Soon...she fell fast asleep. She awoke to the sound of trumpets and cheering crowds in the courtyard below the tower. She sat up and rubbed the sleep from her eyes. Was this a dream? She thought to herself. She shook her head and threw her hair behind her shoulders, jumper up to the window to see the crowd below. There, riding in the front with the general was her lover. Her joy was over whelming; her heart began to pound as if she had run a foot race in the courtyard when she was yet a child. Would he come to her? Would he remember her and long for her kiss at first sight?

She raced down the spiraled stairwell running as fast as her feet could carry her, "I must get to our meeting place as fast as I can...surely he will come to me," she said to herself as she ran. She arrived at the main hallway of the court, she looked, and all the citizens' attentions were to the font gates. She ran across the hall and down to the lower chamber to await her lover. She waited. Finally she heard footsteps moving down the stair to her location. She was waiting in the shadows looking up the stair. At this point she had all but given up. He must have forgotten. Suddenly, she heard her lover call her name in a soft and assuring voice. She ran to his arms and grabbed him; they locked in a passionate kiss. All the emotion of days gone by soon drifted calmly away as if a leaf slowly falling from a tree on a warm fall day, into the glass reflection of a spring fed pool where it slowly floats into the day. Their love seems to be the perfect picture of passion, loyalty, and joyful hope of a life together someday.

This story is one from the creative mind. It may not be the true story of this painting; however, that is the nature of art--it is truly in the eyes of the beholder. No one can say what story was in the mind of the painter of this picture. It could have been a portrait of a love he once had, or, simply the fantasy of what love should be. The message matters not because each passerby, each who stands before the painting to admire its beauty, each who stands before it to interpreting its tale will surely be reminded of the fantasy of the passionate lovers kiss.

3
A LESSON IN LOVE

There we sat, Joanne and I, looking at one another, wondering if we were doing the right thing, trying in some way, once again, to believe we were meant to be--both of us knowing deep down we were not. We were in the office of a county divorce mediator waiting to sign the final papers. God, it was so sad, yet, I knew it was the right thing, I knew we could never work. I wanted it to work; I wanted to think we really loved one another. I wanted to believe that we had missed something, some technique, something somewhere in a Christian counseling book, but no, we had tried it all. We did not have a healthy love or respect and I would not know what that really was for quite some time.

Joanne and I had met while I taught Karate at a local school in Northern Tennessee. I was going through a divorce with my first wife and Joanne was a student of mine. We hit it off right from the start. Joanne was about 5`8"; she had beautiful fine--almost baby-like-- blonde hair. I was never much on blondes but she had that Irish-- spunky--blonde look about her. She had hazel eyes and beautiful red lips that were thin and almost like a china doll. She was curvy and slightly plump but not truly overweight or heavy. She was a beautiful woman and very mysterious in a sexy sort of way.

Joanne had a great sense of humor and we loved to laugh. She was very quick witted. After about nine months of our friendship we went out on a date--there was no turning back. My divorce was soon final and I moved in with Joanne. It was like night and day, and she began to show a neurotic side that became a Jeckle and Hyde story until the end.

I was always a good looking guy and that was actually a curse for me. I abused (emotionally) women and took them for granted my whole life. I never saw (because of my arrogance) the love, devotion, and care some of the women in my life had shown me. I was a heart breaker of the first order--I would soon get my just reward. I would soon understand the pain of a broken heart.

Joanne had a spell over me that I cannot explain to this very day. She was emotionally, mentally, and physically abusive. We were married within two months of my divorce from my first wife; we were in marriage counseling within six weeks of our honey moon. Joanne had two lovely daughters that I adored. The three of them were like carbon copies of one another and I was so proud to have them in my life. I treated her girls like they were my own. Together we had five kids, I had three, and she had the two girls. Joanne was jealous of my kids, in fact, she hated my kids; she was abusive to them in every way possible but did so behind my back. My children were afraid of her and never told me the truth until later in life.

Before I could learn to understand what love is, I had to learn what love is not. Love is not lust, it is not self-serving, it is not a friendship that feels good, and it is not something you hope catches on. Love can develop over time--don`t misunderstand--I just mean to say it should be there from the start, it should have that "it" factor.

Things started to come to a head in the winter of 2004 and I decided one day that I had to leave. I moved in with a friend of mine and I began to see what love was not, I began to have the scales removed from my eyes, and I began to see that if I were to ever really experience true love it certainly would not be with Joanne. Over the next year I learned about my own true neurosis. I learned just how damn crazy I really was and just how far from reality my conception of true love really was. Joanne still held a sick and toxic spell over me; I still at times found myself at her beck and call; in fact, I even moved back in with her twice. It was only after a completely insulting and demeaning Skype conversation with Joanne that something snapped.

She had left on a mission trip to India and the only conversations we had were in the early mornings via Skype. For some reason (I don`t recall) Joanne decided to give me a dissertation on all of my character defects according to her. As I sat there staring at her it was like I slipped into some kind of a dream. I could hear her voice in the back ground like some kind of faint echo. My mind drifted back in time and the memories of her true personality started flowing in faster and faster and suddenly--I was completely disconnected. I just did not care, I was indifferent, I was numb, and I was done. I don`t even know how the conversation ended or if I even said goodbye, I just closed my laptop, walked outside, jumped on my Harley, and drove away.

I heard an old saying one time that I have found to be true, "when the student is ready the teacher will appear." I was a piece of raw clay. I was a blank slate. I was a student of all that was wrong about love, I needed a teacher, the student was definitely ready, and God sent into my life a true teacher, a true love that I would never imagine I could have.

While I was separated and going through my divorce (living in the basement of my best friend's house) his sister who lived upstairs had a friend who moved in because she was divorcing her husband of fourteen years. Apparently, the guy smoked some crack one day at a party and never looked back. She was a very quiet young woman and I never saw her much to start with. Occasionally my friend's sister would invite me up for dinner and I would see her and talk to her. She really was an angel and I felt so badly for her and her situation. Ellen was her name.

Ellen was about 5`5" and had a very slim build. She had dark almost black long hair, very white creamy skin with slight freckles, dark brown eyes, and wide puffy red lips. She wore classes like you would see on a librarian, you know, the kind with pointed rims. She honestly looked like she was about twenty-two but I found out later she was in her mid-thirties. Most of the time when she would come to the table she would be knitting as we sat and talked, she had a calm, wise, demeanor about her, and I soon learned she was a very devout Christian. I never heard her speak ill of anyone or curse. I had to watch my sailor's mouth when I was around her. She was almost a nerd but not quite. We soon realized we were both in the same boat and we became friends.

Ellen and I started to become very close friends over the next year; I have to admit that I never once thought of her as a girlfriend or had any interest in dating her. I would cry on her shoulder about Joanne and she would always listen. We watched movies together and ate ice cream at midnight; we shared our fears, our pain, and our joy almost daily. I began to feel that I truly loved this woman, and that she loved me as well. I don`t mean romantic love--I was not there yet--I mean genuine care, genuine concern, and genuine respect--genuine love.

Within a year I was divorced from Joanne. Ellen and I had become so close that we soon decided to go on an official date. I remember our first kiss and our first embrace. I remember the moment that I knew we were in love. For the first time in my life I had a partner who thought like I did, who shared my interests, who believed in the same things I believed in, and who was loyal and trustworthy. We use to tell people we were like peanut butter and jelly, we just naturally fit. Ellen taught me what real love is, and showed me every day by her actions. I found out that love truly is a verb and that actions speak louder than words. We are still together today and live a quiet happy life. She is an artist and a part time librarian. I am a freelance writer and together we truly are living happily ever after. I finally learned what true love is and what it is not.

4

THE TAX COLLECTOR

Zachariah set by the bedside of his uncle as he slept. His uncle was very ill and on his death bed. He loved his uncle and did not know what he would do when his uncle was gone. Zachariah would not leave his side; he stroked his uncle`s hair and held his hand. He had lived with his uncle since he was about five years old--his mother and father were jailed as zealots by the Romans and he had not seen them since that day. His uncle Eliezer, a wealthy tax collector, took him in.

His uncle had been a tax collector in the city of Bethlehem for many years until something changed him. Zachariah remembered that day a few years back because it was the beginning of a very pleasant and wonderful life with his uncle Eliezer who became a very different man.

Zachariah had always loved his uncle but his job as a tax collector had made him cold hearted, shrewd, and friendless. The only thing his uncle Eliezer cared about besides Zachariah was his money and his standing with the Roman leadership in Bethlehem. Zachariah sat by his uncle`s bed that night and recalled the day his uncle came home to tell him a strange story that changed his uncle--both of their lives were never the same from that day forward.

Zachariah`s mind drifted back five years ago to a December night when his uncle came bursting through the front door:

"Zachariah! Zachariah! Are you here?"

"Yes uncle--I`m here in my room"

"Come quickly" his uncle replied

"Yes uncle, what is it?"

Zachariah had never seen his uncle act this way. He seemed very excited, his eyes were filled with a fiery flair, and he seemed completely consumed with an exuberance Zachariah had never seen from him before. His uncle was normally a quiet, reserved, and emotionless man. He was usually direct, to the point, and never seemed happy about much of anything and he certainly never came through the door like this. His uncle worked hard and never socialized much. Their lives were centered on work, money, and more work; his uncle was very attentive to him but was never one to give compliments or small talk. Eliezer loved Zachariah but constantly stayed on him about his lack of discipline and work ethic. But tonight, something was different, something had changed, his uncle was acting in a way Zachariah had never seen before--Zachariah was concerned.

"Uncle...are you ok?" Zachariah asked with a slight tremble in his voice.

"Yes, yes Zachariah...I`m fine...I must tell you what I have seen!"

His uncle sat him down and began to tell him a strange story about what he had experienced that night. He told Zachariah that he had been walking from the tavern in Bethlehem when he saw a group of people staring up at a strange new star that, until that very night, no one had seen before in the skies above Bethlehem. Eliezer told Zachariah that he walk over to the group out of curiosity and began to listen to their questions and theories about this new star in the sky. There were others, his uncle said, who were speaking of a group of people who saw some wealthy dignitaries and wise men from other countries, along with their soldiers, who had come to Bethlehem by following the star. No one knew why they were here and some even spoke of a rebellion against the Roman occupation during the census. Eliezer wanted no part of any zealot plots to overthrow Rome, but, he was curious to see what this was all about. He told Zachariah that something drove him outside of his normal comfort level—he felt unusually compelled to go to this cave.

Eliezer said he decided to follow the crowd down the road just outside of town to the cave in the hills. He told Zachariah that the star seemed to shine right down on this cave and that there was a large group of people standing around the cave; there were Sheppard's, towns people, Rabbi`s, and all manner of people. He told Zachariah that he pushed his way forward in the crowd until he could see in the cave.

"What did you see uncle...what was in the cave?" Zachariah asked.

"It was the most extraordinary thing but I did not yet understand it." His uncle replied.

"I saw three exotic looking men, very well dressed, almost like they were Kings and a small group of the town leaders standing around a child who had just been born"

"I was not sure why they were standing there or who this child was."

"I tried to ask several people about the child but they did not answer me"

"He was in a feeding troth, wrapped in ragged blankets, and his mother and father seemed to me to be simple peasants."

"The people...they were just standing there staring at the child, almost as if in a trance." His uncle said.

"Was this child someone special?" Zachariah asked.

This question seemed to disturb Eliezer; he turned to the window and was silent for a while—he seemed to be in deep thought. His uncle seemed to fall into a trance and he remained still and quiet for some time. Suddenly, He turned and looked at Zachariah as if he was very frightened, and yet, he said nothing. Zachariah became concerned again and could not figure out what could possibly have frightened his uncle so--he knew his uncle to be a fearless man. He sat with his uncle and did not say a word but he could no longer stand to see him look this way:

"Uncle, what is it?"

"Are you ok?"

"What happened to you?"

"Uncle!"

Eliezer finally turned to him, his eyes fixed like a laser glaring into Zachariah`s soul, then, he began to tell him what happened next. He told Zachariah that he was not sure what he was seeing. He asked a few people in the crowd but they all just shushed him and turned back to stare at the child. He said that finally one man told him the child was a king--the new King of the Jews. He told Zachariah that it made no sense to him and he decide to leave this nonsense behind him and return home before the Romans came to break up this treasonous gathering. Eliezer had seen once before what happens to zealots and wanted no part of such talk about a "New King."

He explained that as he walked back up the hill toward town he was suddenly in the presents of a bright light, his body was frozen, and he fell to the ground on his face in total shock and fear. Eliezer said the in spite of his fear he noticed an overwhelming fragrance of beautiful flowers, the night air was suddenly warm as if it were summer again, and the ground he lay on felt almost hot. He said he was terrified and could not move. Suddenly, he heard a voice as loud as thunder:

"Eliezer!"

"Eliezer!"

"Where are you going?" said the voice.

Eliezer said he wanted to run or crawl away but his body was frozen, he could not move a muscle.

"Who...who are you?" replied Eliezer.

"I am an Angel of the Lord your God who is sent to watch over the child."

"Please, please, don`t kill me...I have done nothing wrong. I am a tax collector but I have always been fair and honest" said Eliezer.

"Do not fear Eliezer for the Lord God in heaven has chosen to reveal a thing to you tonight that you may be of service unto his Kingdom."

"Me...What...what is it I must do?" Eliezer replied in fear.

"The child you have seen this night is the son of the living God, sent to take upon him the sins of the world." said the Angel.

"This night you have seen the Lamb of God, the King of all kings, the messiah of whom the Prophets have spoken."

"Believe on him and you shall have everlasting life."

"You shall live the remainder of your days in service to God`s people in his land."

He told Zachariah that as he lay there face down, still afraid to move, the light slowly faded and was gone. Eliezer said that he slowly stood up and he knew at once he must return to the cave. Eliezer said he walked back to the cave and watched as the strangers from foreign lands gave the child gifts and prayed over him and then he left and came home.

"Zachariah...the messiah has come and we must be prepared to follow him someday." His uncle said.

"What is his name?" asked Zachariah.

"His name is Jesus" his uncle replied.

His uncle Eliezer was never the same from that day forward. He never collected taxes again and he used his wealth to help others in the community. Every year on the anniversary of that day his uncle Eliezer would hold a special dinner in honor of the coming King. His uncle would always give a small gift to those who came to the dinner--he said it reminded him of God`s gift to the world that December night.

Zachariah returned his thoughts to his uncle lying next to him in the bed. He wished his uncle could stay and see the coming King in all his glory.

Suddenly, Eliezer raised his head and grabbed Zachariah with both hands on his cheeks. His eyes were weak and his breath very shallow--slowly, and in a faint voice, he spoke his final words to Zachariah.

"Zachariah, it is time I go to the Kingdom." His uncle said.

"You must take your belongings and follow this Jesus when I am gone."

"He is God`s greatest gift of mercy to mankind...he is the messiah."

"Yes Uncle, I will do as you say." Zachariah replied.

His uncle lay back down, closed his eyes, and passed on.

5
WHAT A DIFFERENCE A DAY MAKES

Have you ever awakened in the morning and felt that it was going to be a fantastic day only to have it turn into absolute hell within moments? It`s kinda like some, some...thing just grabbed you and threw you into some parallel universe of which you can`t escape. It`s like when you're in a dream and you need to run but your legs won`t move. Let me give you a scenario:

You wake up and head out to the porch, maybe, like me, you have an awesome place like a screen porch where you like to sit and read or do a morning meditation or whatever. You sit down, the sun is just cresting the horizon, you sip a delicious cup of your favorite coffee and crack open your bible or some other favorite book. You look down at the bird feeders and they are full of every kind of bird: Cardinals, Chickadee`s, Titmouse`s, Doves, Blue Jays....aaaaah, what a beautiful morning you think to yourself.

All at once: the dog starts barking, the cell phone rings, the kids run through the screen door fighting. You jump up, and as you do, your coffee spills and burns the hack out of your leg and stains your favorite book. As you try to catch the cup before it breaks--it`s your favorite in the collection of course—you knock your computer off the table and sure enough it lands in the spilled coffee as well. As you bend over to grab the computer, before the coffee soaks into the keyboard, the dog runs through your legs causing you to lose balance and you fall through the screen on the porch and land in the rose bushes--OUCH! At this point you`re lying on the ground, you can`t move, and you look up at the sky and say, "What just happened?"

The wonderful thing about life is that it is full of new experiences, some bad, some good, but all are worthwhile--I know, I just told myself to shut up too *laughing*.

You lay there and wonder what life would be like if you had a rewind button kinda like that move "Click" with Adam Sandler where he has the universal remote control and he fast forwards and rewinds his life at will. I have actually went to "Bed Bath and Beyond" looking for that very remote myself. I have went through so many days like this where I just decided that today is gonna suck and that`s that. I loved the movie "Lethal Weapon" with Mel Gibson when his partner played by Danny Glover said, "I think God hates me," to which Gibson reply`s, "hate him back, it works for me."

I swear I can relate so much to that because that is exactly how I lived my life especially when things went to hell in a hand basket in short order. I was so pissed because life wasn`t going my way, people were not doing what they should be doing, things were not organized in my fashion, and, the players in the play did not know their part. As Shakespeare once said, "All the world is a stage." The difference is that I am not always the director.

I have to admit I went through a near breakdown mentally trying to control the world, didn`t they know who I was? If only people, places, and things would subscribe to the wisdom of William all would be well. I knew at once the answer would be to write a book about life: "Life according to William," and then: New York Times best sellers list, a book signing tour, new book deals, a movie, a life of leisure with a new screen porch, no dogs, and no damn kids *laughing*.

I had a wise old friend of mine, no it wasn`t some 90 year old Indian chief who just happened into my life with the wisdom of Solomon and the patience of Job, he was just an old country gentlemen that I liked to eat breakfast with at the local greasy spoon. He was about 85, I think, at the time and I asked him what he thought was the secret to living long. He looked at me as though he could see right through my soul, as if the cosmos had placed he and I together right then at that moment in time, as if--forgive my narcissism--his whole purpose in life was to give me a message. Ok, it really didn`t go down like that but I thought it would make for a good read. Anyway, he looked at me and said, "William my boy, I just never worry about stuff that I can`t change."

That`s it!!--I thought to myself--those are the words of wisdom I have been waiting for thirty plus years to hear? I was pissed. Then he looked at me and added, "I decided a long time ago that if stuff wern`t goin my way, I`d have to accept it, and if my day started off wrong...I could start it over anytime I wanted to."

I went home that day and I started thinking about what the old man said. Start my day over. That thought penetrated my mind, it was simple, it was pure, and it was almost crystal clear. I thought back to the thousands of times I blew my lid, cussed out the kids, kicked the dog; shot the mailman a bird because he delivered one of those dreaded pink envelopes to me; none of my words, actions, or thoughts ever changed anything that happened--except my insurance premium for high blood pressure. I realized the simple fact that I could not change people, places, or things, but I could change my attitude about them. I know what you`re thinking; I should have placed a "BARF" warning in the previous paragraph, but seriously, we have the power to change our thoughts, we have the power to start our day over, we have the power to let go and let God.

6
AMENDS

In life we will make our share of mistakes, and in some cases, the same mistake more than once. The human ego is a horrible task master which demands our undying loyalty. It tells us things are just fine, we are ok, we did nothing wrong, and they deserved it. The ego blinds us to the truth which may set us free, it tells us: "No... don`t look there" when in fact, we desperately need to look. The human ego is in most cases a liar who has our worst interest at heart disguised by a mask of self-defense. There have been millions of untold stories of destruction and failure in the human experience which falls at the feet of the human ego.

When we hurt another person we are at once left with two choices: To let it go, or, try and make it right again. I am speaking strictly about when we hurt someone and we know we have hurt them or they told us that we have hurt them. It is in those cases that we must make a choice which will ultimately cause a war with our ego. The first thing that takes place is that our mind races to defend itself; it looks for anything to explain the situation in a way that will place the blame somewhere else or in another direction. The mind is now in total defense mode and focuses totally on that end, forgetting completely, the person who may have really been hurt.

The human ego has its purposes and some of them are useful and good; it can drive us to great success and invention; it can give us the strength and will to fight and win; however, it can also turn us in the wrong direction and cause a past full of wreckage we must someday clean up. Cleaning up this wreckage is what I hope to address. I hope to share some experience, strength, and hope in this matter.

What is an apology? What is an amends? What do they really mean? How do I take these actions correctly? These are some of the questions a person may have, that is, if they are really looking for answers and have a true desire to set matters straight. In making an amends we must first recognize our ego may be lying to us and not allowing us to see the offense which occurred in the proper light. When our defenses go up we are immediately thinking of ourselves and not truly able to focus on the other persons feelings or see their side of it. This is where the true cross roads of an amends are found.

If we can stop our ego--at that moment--from telling us we have done no wrong or that we must not look there, we can truly listen to the offended person and hear their complaint. It shows more wisdom to stop and listen to something we may not want to hear rather than to spiral into a mode of self-defense and excuses. At this point, if we pass this test of human ego, we can truly focus and hear the person's complaint and have a shot at righting the wrong which may have occurred.

What does the word "amends" mean? The dictionary makes it clear that it is an act of change, a mending of ways, setting things back to the way they were before the offense occurred. If we truly desire to make an amends, if we truly care about the feelings of others, if we sincerely want to make things right again, we must take action. We must give a sincere apology and then set out to rectify the situation by making things the way they were prior to the offense if possible. This is an action step that requires work on our part; if we are unable to set things back the way they were we must change our behavior which is the action step in that case.

Furthermore, when making an amends, we must not bring up anything that we think they may have done to us at that point. It is not an amends to say something like, "I am sorry, but I would not have done [it] if you had not done...`Fill in the blank'" This is an example of ego being in the way. It is an example of placing blame on the actions of others rather than taking responsibility for our side of the street. There is no room for a "but" after the words "I am sorry" if we truly want to make an amends. An old proverb makes a valid point which states: "Even a fool is counted wise when he remains silent." In some cases an amends may consist of us shutting our mouth and just listening to the other person's grievance; in some cases the person simply wants to be heard. The point of this is to say that a true amends requires an act of selflessness that is very much in conflict with the human ego. May God bless your efforts.

7

THE COUNTRY STORE

Wisdom is sometimes allusive. I find myself learning some of life's greatest lessons when I least expect it, or in some cases, when I don`t even know it. Sometimes, when we are not looking for it or thinking about it, wisdom presents itself to us. It is sometimes laid at our feet in disguise, looking like a stone when in fact it is a pearl of great price.

There is a store I stop at quite often. The store is an old country store that is family owned and has been for decades. This old store sets nestled back in a little curve on a beautiful mountain road. The front of the store has the old "Mountain Dew" drink signs, old tools, horse saddles, and all that you would expect to see at such a store. There is an old church pew in the front that the locals use to chew the fat in the early mornings and late evenings. The old bench has names carved in it, bubble gum stuck to it, and the burn marks of cigarettes and cigars.

Most of the time when I come to the store I can expect to see "Buck," an elderly black man who lives about two miles up the mountain. Buck is a sweet old man and I love to listen to his stories when I have time. I sometimes just sit and listen to the stories of the past and his views on life. Since I was a boy I have always loved elderly people and I love to hear their stories. Little did I know that buck was about to place a pearl of wisdom at my feet that I am thankful I received.

Buck began to tell me a story that morning about his daily walks to the store and the beauty of God's creation along the way. He said that God had given him the gift of discernment as a young man and that he trusted the gut feelings it gave him in his life. He went on to say that these gut feeling were almost always right and had saved his life on some occasions and on other occasions had at least saved him heartache. He said at the beginning of the week he had a feeling there was a bag of money on the side of the road that he would find. He said "I don`t know if I needs it or wat I wud do with it if I found it, I jus felt like the lord was tellin me ta look fur it".

He said he walked the two miles every day looking at the ground on the side of the road. He said he only looked up to watch a passing car or to see how close he was to the store. Every day the same routine looking searching but not finding this bag that was supposed to be there. Finally, buck said it hit him that sometimes his discernment was not right and maybe he had just made a mistake. He said sometimes his own wants became something he thought was a message from God, when in fact; it was just his own selfish desires. He then told me something that has stuck in my head to this day. Buck said, "I finally realized I spent my days lookin fur the money and had missed all a Gods beautiful sites. I spent all my time searchin fur somethin that wasn`t there and missed what was right in front of me."

I thought about what buck had said for days. I realized the message for me was clear: When I take my focus off God and become obsessed with something, I will miss the beauty of Gods gifts that are all around me daily.

8
TO FIND WISDOM

Life, in general, is a walk through a multitude of experiences. Some of us have years and years of pleasant, successful, and productive experiences while others find life to be quite the opposite. Each person has to learn to walk, run, eat, make a living, and love, along with other vital actions needed in our arsenal of tools to survive life and be a success. From the day we are born until the day we die we are constantly learning new ways to deal with life, other people, our family, our business relationships, and other important areas of our existence here on Earth. Wouldn`t it be nice to have an instruction manual?

In any endeavor we decide to proceed with, usually, we can find instruction--whether it is in a manual or another person's advice. This is a choice we can make in each separate endeavor if we choose to look for instruction. In life there is always someone who has been where we want to go, or in some cases, where we have to go. In the Holy Bible the book of Ecclesiastes makes a simple statement of the conditions in life we will face:

What has been will be again,
what has been done will be done again;
there is nothing new under the sun. (Ecclesiastes 1:9)

This leads to an important point: A mentor, a counselor, or an advisor are all available to anyone who would seek to live by wisdom rather than life`s brutal experience. Why would anyone want to go through life making the same mistakes others have made for the simple reason that they had a lack of good council? The only possible answer is that a person who chooses to learn from brutal, raw, experience rather than the wisdom of others does so either out of naiveté or sheer ego. Some people in this world have truly never thought to seek council; others feel they are so talented they need no council, and some, may have sought the wrong council and given up. What is good council, what is a mentor, and where does one find such people?

No matter the circumstance or challenge a person may face--others have been there and know the best path to take. The best metaphor is the mine field: If you had to walk through a mine field would you rather be the first or the last to walk through? If you are looking to start a business, make a change in your personal life, or perhaps facing an incurable disease--someone else has been there and knows the way. The first thing to do is make a determination of what you need council on. The next step is to find someone who has been successful by the fruits they bear in their life--not by their words--and ask for their help. The Bible says, "you shall know a tree by the fruit it bears." This is the best way to find a good councilor; find someone who has what you want, who lives like you want to live, who acts the way you want to act, and who has the business success you want to have, or, the marriage you want for you and your wife.

Most people who are successful (and have fruit in their life to show this success) are happy to share their knowledge with an apprentice who wants to learn. It is true that in some cases mentors want to charge for their services; however, there are those who simply want to give back to society and will do so for free. Think of the vast wealth of knowledge that may be only a phone call or question away from being at your disposal. The use of a mentor or councilor may save thousands of dollars and countless hours of time when taking on a task or setting a goal in life. In short: sit down and think about what it is you want to do in life or what you are facing; find someone who has the fruit of success or the knowledge of the correct path to take and ask for their council. Seek to gain wisdom--not experience.

9
LEANN

There is nothing as painful as the reality of deep dark loneliness, and that is how Leann felt that cold winter day as she waited for the news. Leann had been so close to her grandmother and now that her grandmother was in the hospital she didn`t know what she would do. Leann had no real father in her life and her mother didn`t seem to care. It all started back in July when LeAnn was out of town with her grandmother and she was complaining of a horrible pain in her head. They cut the trip short and headed home early so her grandmother could go and see the doctor.

As the car pulled away from Leann's house she already missed her gramma, she hoped that gramma was ok as she lay down to take a nap. The next day she was told by her mother that gramma was admitted to the hospital and that she would take her to see gramma after work. Later that afternoon Leann watched the clock and wondered where her mother was. The time began to slip away into the evening: 6 o`clock...6:15...6:45, and still LeAnn waited. Leann walked outside and sat on the porch. She began to think back to fond memories of gamma's house. One of her favorite memories was at thanksgiving when gramma always made her favorite peach cobbler, she missed her so bad. Suddenly, her mother's car pulled into the driveway and hit the bush next to the garage--LeAnn knew that her mom was drunk again.

Leann ran off the porch and down the street as her mother screamed obscenities at her telling her to come back. Leann knew that something was wrong with gramma she felt it deep in her soul and she had to see her. As she walked down the street and cried an older women was coming toward her and stopped her. The old women asked her if she was ok and LeAnn told her about her gramma and fell on her shoulder and cried. The old women took her home to her house and gave her hot chocolate, and--to LeAnn's surprise--she had peach cobbler. As they talked the women told LeAnn not to worry that her gramma would be ok in the end and that she was headed for the kingdom.

Leann asked the women what she meant by "The kingdom." The old women told her the story of Jesus of Nazareth and how he had come to heal the broken hearted and set free the captive hearts. The women asked her if she knew about this Jesus and LeAnn said she had heard gramma talk about him, but said she just never went to church with her gramma. That night LeAnn got on her knees with the old women and prayed; she felt more at peace than she had ever felt before and she knew somehow that things would be ok. Leann felt a deep sense that no matter what happened she would see gramma again and she fell fast asleep as the old women stroked her hair.

Leann woke up the next day and she was in her own bed. She jumped up and looked at the clock--it was 9 AM. She ran to the kitchen and picked up the phone and called her mother and asked her about her gramma. Leann dropped the phone as her mother told her the news--her gramma was gone--she had died from an aneurism that night. Leann remembered what the old women had told her the night before, and she lay down on the couch and cried. As LeAnn lay on the couch she heard a knock on the door…she slowly looked up and saw the old women's face looking in. Leann got up and let her in and fell into her arms sobbing.

The old women prayed for her as she lay in her lap on the couch. "Father God have mercy on this your child; give her your peace and surround her with your Holy Spirit…Amen." The women stayed with LeAnn and told her about the kingdom and how happy her gramma would be. She told Leann that she had a new life and would never hurt again. She told LeAnn about her grandmother's mother and father and how they were in the kingdom and she would see them again. Leann began to feel happy for her gramma and once again a peace fell over her and she no longer felt alone. The old women gave LeAnn a bible that seemed very old and special to the women. Leann told her she would read it every day and treasure it for life. The old women hugged her and told her she must go home; her work was done and she was in need of rest. She told LeAnn if she ever needed her again, to just get on her knees and pray, and she would come and see her and comfort her again. Leann thought what the women said was a bit odd but said she would and the old women left.

Leann never saw her again; she tried to remember where the women's house was but couldn't quite seem to remember how to get there. She searched for the women many times over the years and was never able to find her house. Leann grew up and became a children's Sunday school teacher in her church; she never forgot the old women who comforted her at her time of need and told her about Jesus. Leann spent the rest of her life telling people about the kingdom and how they too could find the way there.

10
WADE

The west was hard for most men: The rugged terrain and hot sun blazing down without mercy; but not for wade, he was just hard, plain hard to the core. Wade never cared about nothing--no family, no women, and no cause. Wade was never one to join anything or give a damn about company; he liked being alone and he loved the trail. He loved a good cup of black coffee over a fire and piece of salt covered jerky. Wade loved his pipe, and a good drink of whiskey, and he didn`t mind makin his livin killin men.

He was on his way to Yuma to find some dude that was in the way of a cattle baron`s waterin hole. What did he give damn about cattle or expanding the west--but hell, there was money in it for wade in the form of getting rid of problems. He laid down that night, drank his last sup of whiskey, and put his pipe out, tomorrow was gonna be a long ride.

The next mornin wade loaded up his pack horse, lit his pipe, and hit the trail. Wade had killed some 13 men as best folks could remember, and this one had a good price on his head. The cattle baron told wade he`d pay $5000 to see this man dead; $2500 up front, and the other half when the job was done. Hell, Wade could retire after this one.

Wade rode in to the outskirts of Yuma that evenin, he wasn`t much for bein seen, he kinda liked layin low in a new town with a job that needed doin--his kinda work didn`t need no extra attention. Wade spent the next two days scoutin out the dudes place, learnin his habits, and lookin for his chance to take care a thing`s. Wade noticed the dude went out to the back side of the barn every mornin about 6am. It looked to wade like a grave site from where he was watchin but he couldn't quite tell. Wade decide to make his move the next morning; he'd be a waitin for the dude just behind the barn in an old brush pile.

Wade was fast as lighnin with his colt and always liked to give the man he was killin a chance to draw. Wade told a feller one time it kinda made things right in his mind after it was done. The one thing on this job that was di'fernt was this was a family man and Wade was more use t'a killin trail bums, gunfighters, and cowboys. Wade didn't much care tho cuz this one was payin enough to let him retire.

Wade saw the dude comin out to the grave site bout quarter t'a six that morning; he waited till the dude got 'bout 20 paces from the grave and wade--jumped out--stood up straight, and looked him dead in the eye. The dude froze--lookin damn scared--and said, "can I help ya mister?" Wade answered back and said, "sorry to tell ya friend, you're in the way a progress and I gotta get ya outta the way." The dude stood and looked at wade for what seemed like hours--he knew he had to draw, but all he could think of was his young son.

What wade didn't know was that the dude had lost his wife a few weeks back when the baron sent out some cowboys to take care of business; seems that one of the men made a mistake and shot the dudes wife instead. Their boy was all the dude had left t'a live fur. Now here he was...starring straight down the barrel of colt 45 and no chance a getting out of it without a fight.

BANG!! The sound of a gun blazed through the early morning air and echoed up through the hills---and suddenly, Wade tilted over and fell to the ground. The dude stood shocked--he froze in his tracks— who? what?...suddenly he heard a voice say: "Paw...are you ok?" The dude swung around and there was his boy standin there with a Winchester lowered down. They ran to each other and dropped the iron they both held, they embraced, it was over, and the stranger was dead.

I ben sheriff in Yuma for 20 years all told. I seen a lot a bad men come and go. I ain't never heard a Wade before he come through, but I learn't his story from others who knew him. The one thing an outlaw with a fast gun better never under-estimate in these parts is the love of a family--the love between father and a son. That young boy took down one of the meanest SOB's these parts has ever known; love knows no fear and love will stand up to all things. Love will rule the day.

11
LOVE IS IN THE LITTLE THINGS

John was running late for his plane; the flight was scheduled to leave Atlanta at 4:15 PM and it was 2 PM now. He wanted to see Peggy his wife before he left. "where is she damn it," he exclaimed with a grimace. Peggy was usually home from the office on Tuesdays just after lunch, and besides, she knew her husband was leaving for Chicago after 1:00. John looked at the clock again and again as if watching it closely he could somehow stop the time. He decided to double check his luggage--"if she`s not here by 2:15 I`ve gotta hit the road" he said, as if begging the clock to somehow retrieve his wife from where ever she was.

Meanwhile, Peggy was racing down the road looking at her watch, fists tight around the wheel and eyes focused on the road as she sped forward. "Oooh shoot...I am gonna miss him, I knew I shouldn`t have taken that last call." She hated not being there to see her husband off when he went out of town. The year before their marriage was on the rocks; the kids were gone and they had just somehow grown apart. They were contemplating a separation when their high school buddies and neighbors Mike and Linda suffered a horrible tragedy--Mike was killed in a head on collision.

The accident had a profound effect on them. They both knew at that moment in the kitchen when they received the news about Mike that they never wanted to lose one another, and how blessed they were. There they stood in the kitchen--their eyes locked—and then, they slowly began to walk toward one another and they reached for each other with a deep sense of loss, regret, and sadness for where they had been. They embraced for what seemed like an hour and then slowly walked to the den and sat by the fire. They slept there together that night in each other's arms.

John looked at his watch, and then the kitchen clock, "damn I guess I will just give her a call on the cell and let her know I love her." John headed out to the car, threw his luggage in the rear, and sped away toward the airport--Peggy was only 5 miles from home but she felt deep in her heart she had missed him. Suddenly, her mind--as it often did--raced back to the night Linda got the news about Mike. Her heart raced and she felt a little panicked that she had not looked her man in the eye and kissed him goodbye—"ring, ring, ring," Peggy's cell began to ring from her purse so she pulled over, "maybe that's john," she said in a hopeful tone.

"Hello" answered Peggy.

"Hey honey, I waited as long as I could--where are you?" John said with a hint of frustration.

"I am so sorry honey, I took one more call on that deal we have going on in Roswell--ooooh, I wanted to see your handsome face and …John…I love you."

"I love you too Peggy…don`t worry hun…I will be home in two days and we will spend Saturday together in the Mountains."

John was so tired that night after the meeting. He had closed the big sale that day and was just about to sit and enjoy a good cigar. He sat and thought of how much he missed Peggy. He went to get his night cloths on and as he opened his suitcase he smelled perfume.

"Peggy must have used my bag again or spilled some perfume in here" he thought to himself.

As he dug a little further he saw a white hanky and a note. He picked up the hanky and he immediately recognized the sweet smell of Peggy; she had put her hanky in the suitcase with John's favorite perfume on it. A note was wrapped in the hanky: "John…I love you, always, forever, and no matter what…Peggy."

12
THE VASE

A woman is like a beautiful vase that a man must protect with his very life. Once the vase is cracked or broken, it can be repaired, but it will never be the same.

There once was a man who had a beautiful woman—and yet, he did not understand how precious and fragile her heart could be. She was so in love with him that he knew she would always be there for him.

At first, he spent every day caring for her needs and he cherished their every moment together; she was the only woman he had ever truly loved.

As time went on this man began to take her love for granted; he forgot how truly precious she was to him. He was never there on the nights she cried or when she was lonely and needed his love. He forgot to take the time to appreciate her gentle care for their home and for his every need.

This beautiful woman loved him so much. She cherished his heart and left him without a want or care. She was a woman who knew how to love her man; everything in her being sought to please him and care for him. In life, any fire--no matter how strong or high--can become cold and die.

Love is just like a burning fire which has flames that rise higher, become stronger, and the heat of those flames increases as fuel is added to the fire. The hotter the flames the more it burns its fuel; If no fuel is added to the fire it will soon burn out and turn to ash.

If a man continues to take from the one he loves--but never gives in return--he is letting the fuel that the fire so desperately needs burn down; he is letting his lover's heart grow cold, and the love she once had begins to die out.

One day the man came home and his love was not there; he called her name and searched the house but she was gone. At first he was angry that she dared to worry him so; he wondered how she could be so cold as to leave without a care!

He walked to their bedroom and saw it was empty--she was gone!

On the other side of the room was a night stand with a vase on it that he had once brought to her full of flowers. The vase had fallen one day and was broken in half; he had glued the vase back for her because she loved it so. For a moment all he could do was stare at the vase. His mind reeled with thoughts--memories began to return...

He leaned against the wall and slowly slid down with his hands upon his checks in despair. His memory went back to a summer day where he sat on the front porch at home with his mother.

"Son" he heard his mother say, "Someday you will find a beautiful woman to love and cherish."

"Remember," she said sternly, "A woman is like a vase my son--a precious vase that you must protect with your life."

"Do not let her heart crack or get broken, or it will never be the same."

He suddenly realized that the "vase" had not only been cracked—it was broken—it was destroyed—it was gone.

POEMS
13
ALONE IN THE NIGHT

The night is quiet, and all I hear is the rain.
The dark is a cold and shapeless void,
how can it life sustain?
Feelings rule the night.

The night is still and has no care,
Emotions rule no thought can bear.
As I lay my head to sleep,
instead my fear comes from the deep.

I sing a song as if to say,
my fears aren't real, I am ok.
I say a verse to keep my head;
instead I feel the pain I dread.

The night is ruled by failures past;
the pain is real , the memories last.
My mind begins to race and spin;
my God, my grace, forgive my sin.

I lay until I see dawns light;
the dark, the void, dispelled by light;
and when the Son I finally see,
A prisoner I'll no longer be.

I watch the clock as it strikes six,
I soon will need another fix.
The night creeps in again to stay;

another prayer that I must pray.

The night is quiet and all I feel is pain.
Another soul it comes to claim.
Someday I hope the past will fade;
Yet--until then, I am its slave.

14
A NIGHT OF SILENT RAIN

At first sign of slumber,
At the brink of silent rain;
The chains are all rolled out,
The worms inside my brain.
Is there peace in this life?
Is there no more pain?
Can one find the slumber?
The guiltless all complain.
As my body holds me down,
I contemplate what is without.
In my mind lives fear and doubt;
Can there be a real way out?
If my mind can find this peace;
My soul will surely sing and shout.

15

WANT

In the darkness of despair,
The selfish want more than their share.
You have yours but where is mine?
By themselves in space and time.

A love is more than they can bear,
Alone again with none to share.
If only they could own the sky;
Would this fill the hole inside?

Want is never satisfied.
Want will keep the pain inside.
Want will drive the mind insane.
Want will fill a soul with pain.

Yes, selfishness and want you see,
Will fill the heart and yet not be,
The way to life, to be set free;
Again I say, but can you see?

16
MY ADVERSARY

How fast you seek to find a way,
To destroy those who live in peace.
Your existence is to each new day,
a search for souls to hells increase.

I saw a sheep grazing unaware;
It jumped and skipped through pastures green.
The forest hides the eyes that glare;
Thick black fur and nostrils gleam.

Tis the beast who drives this thing;
No mercy for the meek he shouts.
Ripping flesh and chains that cling;
Once reached there is no turnabout.

Time goes on toward things that change;
Life will never stay the same.
My enemy seeks to rearrange;
How did he come? What is the name?

All was well, we had good grace;
contentment in the midst of all.
Then comes he who must replace;
He stole goodwill, and made us fall.

Do you think a friend you have?
In this world you must stay awake.

Yes—do you think a friend you have?
The enemy comes, and he will take.

17

I MISS YOU SUSAN DEE

I miss you Susan Dee…
Your smile was special and touched the heart,
Your talents were many, your gifts were sweet.
I remember your paintings, your hats, and your art.
I miss you Susan Dee…

You were a place of safety, a rock, steadfast.
You had been through so many things painful
Now, are you able to forget the past?
I loved you Susan Dee…

Your hand was strong when it needed to be,
Your chin was firm, yet soft, and filled with love.
All pain is now gone, your free!!
I need you Susan Dee…

I remember that November day,
I knew from then you would not stay,
You missed her so and wanted to leave,
Your heart was broken and would always bleed.

I was there when the black horse came,
The fear in our hearts fell down like rain,
Yet you were strong until the end,
You knew the Lord--he was your friend.

I miss you Susan Dee...
Even though I know you are free,
I sometimes wish I were with you,
My selfish needs remain with me.

It seems so far and so long away,
The time when I will once again see your face,
I long for that time, I long for that day.
I love you Susan Dee.

18
I FEAR THE NIGHT

I fear the night,
Dark it is and filled with fright.
I whistle as though I do not care,
Yet, I know the night and I despair.

I fear the night.
It surrounds my soul.
Darkness creeps and swirls until,
As black as coal, and deadly still.

I fear the night.
Alone in my bed,
Alone in my soul,
Alone in my head.

I cannot sleep,
Awake I weep,
I ask the Lord my soul to keep.
But still the fear remains so deep.

Yes, I fear the night.
No matter if a verse I say,
No matter if I kneel to pray,
I look forward to the coming day,

Yes, I fear the night.

19
A NEW LOVE

I looked around and for once it was gone,
No longer trapped--no longer its pawn.
I ran through the wind so happy and free;
I whistled in the dark as if no fear would there be.

The dawn showed bright sunlight whose glory brings tears,
A mind twisted with memories of pain through the years.
A new love has come and all will be well;
It opened the gates and released me from hell.

The sheep in a pasture is far from the woods,
Sees not the grey creature whose taste finds him good;
The mind is distracted by thoughts only well,
The outcome uncertain--the future won`t tell.

The beast comes yet closer his smell fills the air;
The innocent gripped with sudden despair.
The choice is now clear, yet late when it's found--
The prey must stay mindful of predators around.

No matter how free and how far and away;
No matter the moments, the years, or the days;
The door must stay closed and the memories gone,
Or find myself--once again--in the game as your pawn.

20

MEMORIES OF SPRING

Chirping birds that fly and play,
Time change makes a longer day.
Green grass shoots and flowers bloom;
No more of winters cold or gloom.

Squirrels and bees and buds on trees,
Sunny days with gentle breeze,
Smell the blooms and fresh cut grass;
Joy rushing in--its spring at last!

Carpenter bees fly around,
New growth covers the once cold ground.
Rainey days replenish the land,
The master's creation, so beautiful, so grand.

Spring time evenings, tranquil and still;
Sunsets slowly over the hill.
Frogs and crickets sing a song;
The owl and whippoorwill sing along.

I lay myself down--alone in my bed;
Spring time memories run through my head.
I fold my hands and begin to pray;
I thank my God for another day.

21
A CHRISTMAS PAST AND PRESENT

The desert sands blew across the land,
A star shown down, the makers hand.
The Angel spoke, "do not fear,"
"A child is born, your king is here."

In his father`s will he vowed and lived,
A child, a man, our God did give.
Alone and in pain his live he gave,
defeating death and hell, the grave.

As time flows forward like ocean waves,
The king still lives--the King who saves.
The presents lay around the tree,
reminding souls they are set free.

The leaves turn orange, yellow and red.
"It`s raining leaves," the young child said
The wind and rain begin to blow,
at Christmas time it turns to snow.

Lights and bulbs colored green and red,
"Merry Christmas" the father said.
Turkey dinner, cookies and bread,
Santa is coming tonight in his sled.

Christmas is merry a time full of cheer,
children and presents, one`s family is near.

As time slowly passes we should never forget,
The Lamb who was spotless that paid the full debt.

22
TO A FRIEND

A friend is like a ring of gold,
Its value known by those who hold.
Friends are few and far between--
Loyal, true, opinions keen.

On dark nights when tears oft flow;
At times in life nowhere to go.
A heart that`s broke and cannot heal;
To give advice--a love that`s real.

Always there in times of need;
Healing wisdom, words to heed.
The brightest star within the sky;
No price to pay, no reason why.

A sack of Gold within his hand,
The stranger walked into the land.
To buy and sell, or some to lend;
And yet, the gold brought him no friend.

In a life where things can rust--
Where all must die--return to dust;
There is no thing which one can hold,
Except a friend worth more than gold.

If you find this precious gift;

That friend who truly spirits lift.
Do not betray--do not forget!
For those who do will long regret.

23
MANS BEST FRIEND

Soft fuzzy bellies that roll up to pet
He has no worries, he has no regret
Loving eyes that wait for a glance
A toss of the ball or let out of the fence
Easily pleased and no strings attached
So few friends in life could better be matched
Sits at the door in the morning son`s light
Asleep at the foot of the bed every night
Mustaches, beards, eyebrows and tails
My friend the dog who`s love never fails
On summer days he walks by my side
Or in my old truck he`s along for the ride
For a ball or a bone or a stick he will wait
Never a friend that I`ve had was this great
Someday I`ll wake and my bones will wax cold
Alone in my bed with my life`s story told
My friend the dog will be there by my side
Forever my friend till the day that I die

24
IM STUCK IN HERE

I`m stuck in here!
I cannot move or think...
My feet won`t walk...
I can see but it`s only me.

I can`t get out!
It`s dark and cold and I can`t feel words...
Pain crawls around inside...
There's nowhere to hide!

I`m trapped in here!
Can anyone see what I see?
Or is it just me?
Everything is heavy and moving slow--can I go?

I`m chained and I can`t move!
I have tried so many times to escape...
Why can`t I go?
Hello!!

I`m stuck in here!
Trapped in thoughts that won`t stop,
Trapped in a mind of my own that's blown,
Trapped in a fear that is only in here...

I really can't get out!
I can see inside but not without.

I can't feel anything you say...
Hey!!

They can`t see me!
I can see them--can I flee?
I`m tired--someone help me!
I`m stuck in here...

I will just wait cuz I know my fate,
I will just close my eyes and stop,
I will just curl up and cry...
Do you know why?

...I`m stuck in here!!

25
THE BLUE RIDGE

Mist floats high upon the cool gray sky,
Stillness broken by the red hawks cry,
Dawn breaks slow in the mountains cool,
Dewdrops form into a pool.

Mountain laurel blooms fill the air,
A Nuthatch sings without a care,
Clouds float across like peaceful dreams,
Brook trout play in cold clear streams.

White pines tower, ferns carpet the ground;
Sheer rock faces with waterfalls abound.
Day lilies reach for the sun through the trees;
Blackberries, muscadines, and honeybees.

White tail deer run free and play,
Black bear cubs sleep all day,
Grandfather Mountain reaches higher than most,
Cross her roped bridge and you can boast!

Appalachian Trail runs through its heart,
Through the Blue Ridge Mountains from its start;
Breathe taking beauty for all to see,
The lord and his handy work will ever be.

26
THE MASTER COMES

I missed you--tis true, and my love is yet strong,
My heart skips a beat like notes in a song,
It ponders the heart and the mind is not clear,
The memory brings pain and the eyes shed a tear.

Awake in the dark as I search for what`s right;
The dreams and the thoughts take control of the night.
A song in the distance brings emotion too strong--
A lost lover who sings bout` a love that's gone wrong.

The master still calls me as night is her lair,
I run from the shadow I feel the despair,
I finally give in, as there's nowhere to run;
I must give up the fight as the damage is done.

The morning shines bright and drives away fear,
The night is so lonely, your presents not near.
A welcome return from the night--the abyss!
Yet through all of the pain I still long for your kiss.

I think that I see you in places I go,
I run fast to catch up but it's no one I know,
All of the places which memories surround,
There no place I can go where your ghost is not found.

I dread the suns falling and the night almost here,
Once again I`m a prisoner of shadows and fear,

Your memory commands me like master to slave;
To again kiss your lips is all that I crave.

As the night closes in I hold on to what's dear,
The memories I hold even if you`re not near,
I will treasure you always alone in my bed,
A slave to the master until I am dead...

27
THE OLD DUSTY BOOK

It sits on a shelf
But not by itself
It might collect dust
But never does rust
Yellow are its pages
Passed down through the ages
Its cover is torn
Its back, bent, and worn
How long must it sit?
When last a lamp lit?
How long must it wait?
Must this be its fate?
An old book is wise
Its pages a prize
Its knowledge untold
From memories of old
So walk to the shelf
Be good to yourself
And grab from its nook
An old dusty book

28
SADNESS

A darkness so thick that it can be touched,
No peace of mind is within my clutch,
This love that haunts me steals my soul--
I cry, I beg, I've lost control.

To all others it seems that things are quite well;
Yet still, I live in my own private hell.
And tell me--to what end will all this be?
My heart, it seems, will never be free.

I long to see your smiling face...
I long to be back in that place,
Where love was strong and all was well--
Your body's heat--your touch, your smell.

This fantasy stalks me—it controls my mind,
Reality harsh, the truth is unkind;
For when we were yet not ever apart;
Your love was cold--always crushing my heart.

The magic spell--in trance I stay,
The devils son with me does play,
The mind is cruel and never sound,
A ghost of you has kept me bound.

The nights are yours no sleep is found,
The demons chains rapped all around,
The lovers spell will always be,

A life of pain that won't set free...

The days are bright yet filled with pain,
The sadness rules and falls like rain,
Please let me have a moment free--
Your lovely face I'll never see...

I long for death that will not come,
The only rest, my feelings numb.
Please set me free--release the chains!
The sadness stays, my love remains...

29
THE THORN IN MY SIDE

The mental obsession--
It won`t go away,
It won`t let me go,
It leads me astray...

Help me o` lord, I need to be strong!
My days are so short, my nights are so long.
Do for me lord what I can`t do for myself;
Put me away on some high moral shelf.

I fall on my face and I curl up to pray,
Please take it lord, please keep it at bay.
The mind is locked in, nothing else can I think;
The evil inside gives a laugh and a wink.

I have no control--there is nowhere to run!
The thorn in my side gives off heat like the sun.
I look for some answer, a proverb, a verse--
As the darkness surrounds me a prayer I rehearse.

Then finally it's plain that release must be had;
My soul deep in sadness my addiction so bad.
My fist pounds the table--why can`t I let go?
The thorn in my side makes a prisoner my soul.

The morning sun breaks to yet one more day,
My heart drops like a rock, my senses astray,

William Power

The black hole is deep and it`s end can`t be found,
The thorn in my side--in my misery I`ll drowned.

The darkness returns and the demonic beast,
My flesh is destroyed my soul is its feast,
The heart is no matter my prayers go unheard,
The lord has abandoned—I`ve scoffed at his word!

I awoke in the night to bright light rushing in;
The demons all scurried as they ran from within;
Lighting and thunder, trumpets and wind;
Angelic beings came and took all my sin!

The Lord God Almighty sits high on his throne,
He never forsakes us we are never alone;
No matter how deep or how far or how wide;
The Lord and his mercy took the thorn from my side.

62

30
ESCAPE FROM WRATH

I was there but I escaped,
The gates of hell, the demonic shapes.
The pit is dark and cold and deep--
There is no peace--there is no sleep.

The master's hammer, the bell is rung,
The slaves all gather, the web is spun,
The cock is slain, the deed is done;
They`re all in tears nowhere to run.

The demons gather for the feast,
They celebrate with gnashing teeth,
They wait to move in on the prey,
The beast will come at night to stay.

The chained are cold and steel rips flesh;
There is no warmth in hell`s dark depths.
Creatures stalk with fiery glare;
Their glowing eyes in darkness stare.

No end in sight to all this pain--
The beast is King, all hope in vain.
A virgin on a marble slab;
The demon raised his knife to stab.

Those without become insane,
Those within can feel no shame.

The beast will never let you go;
His mighty reign of pain he`ll show!

The torture goes on night and day;
Countless numbers demons slay.
Worm invested rotting flesh;
A drop of blood, the faith will test.

I woke to find my bed a wreck,
Sweat and tears rolled down my neck,
My heart raced wild, my fear was real--
A nightmare tale my peace did steal.

At once I saw it was a dream;
My mouth was open as if to scream.
My life was once in hells cold grasp;
Forever would my torture last.

The Lord had mercy from on high,
From demons past, from Satan`s lie.
For he loved me so and had a plan;
From a torture son, a brand new man.

31

LOVE HAS BLIND EYES

Her beauty beyond all he had seen,
God had delivered to this man a Queen;
Her lips, they were moist, and longed for his kiss,
This was the man that fulfilled her wish.

Her past had been dark, filled with secrets and pain;
Emotions kept back, will soon fall like rain.
One can`t always see what`s behind someone's eyes--
Silence blankets the soul when it cries.

The plan was a life like none knew before,
God would reveal for them each open door,
The heart truly hides all mysterious things,
The new lovers soared as if on eagle's wings.

Flowered fields, and Blue Mountains tall;
A path, a brook, a cool waterfall.
Lovers will laugh and secrets will keep,
A place to make love, and then peaceful sleep.

He prayed to the Lord--only he could stop time!
I must have all eternity with this Queen who is mine!
But the Lord knew the truth of this love and its end;
The dark side would come and his heart would not mend.

She needed a hero for her demons to slay,
And only for her would the demons give way,

Behind her soft eyes was a heart made of stone,
With demons inside she was never alone.

What once was a dream that could never be wrong,
Now turned to a game in which he was her pawn,
Hell hath no fury as a woman unleashed,
She tore out his heart as if she were a beast.

As winds blew the curtains he awoke in the night--
Was this a nightmare--how could this be right?
He called his Queens name as he ran down the stair;
No voice returned--his Queen was not there!

It seems that the demons demanded her soul;
Her lover, her hero, could not pay their toll.
He tried as he might, but would never forget;
His life drifted on, his heart caught by her net.

His loving eyes, in her saw no wrong.
The dreams that he held for her, turned out all wrong.
His love was his weakness, and eyes--they were blind!
She chained up his heart and imprisoned his mind.

32
DEATH OF A LOVE

It follows me where ever I go--
I push it down and yet it grows;
Some days at best I can forget,
On other days it stalks me yet.

Our love was strong like iron or steel,
Our hearts let go, they did reveal,
We laughed, we sang--we ran, we played,
We kissed, we loved, and slept all day.

What happened next seems so surreal;
It crept in slow, it came to steal.
We felt it near yet couldn`t see,
What it would do to our love so free.

I saw a glimpse of its black robe,
A shadow, a ghost, no face to show,
And then one day to my surprise--
I saw its face, I saw its eyes.

It sought our love,
It would not rest,
It ran us down,
We did our best.

I still look back and wonder why;
The dream still lives and I still cry.

You're in my dreams I cannot sleep
Thoughts of love I`ll ever keep,

The day will come and may be near,
The eyes grow cold, and no more fear;
And I will think upon that day,
Of the death of love one cold fall day.

33
THE BONDAGE OF SELF

Inside a mind filled with despair,
Loneliness abides in the unbridled instinct,
I know well because I have been there,
Relieve me from the bondage of self.

Lift up your eyes—remove the scales,
A heavy heart and darkness reigns,
Cover my ears from cries and wails;
Relieve me of the bondage of self.

Then, a dove landed on my shoulder,
The scales fell like pouring rain.
No more burdens to unfold,
No more self-inflicted pain.

Locked within, disconnected without,
Is a life that is filled with only self,
Tis` filled with fear, pain, and doubt;
Oh God! Save me from the bondage of self.

34
REDEMPTION

Men are born to climb the hill,
To stress, to toil—to lose self-will,
And tell me what is all this for?
Some say to find the kingdom's door.

Standing at the tall sheer wall,
Stories say that men did fall.
They also say what's said before,
They found their way to Heaven's door.

We fight; we win--then lose again,
From mother's womb where life begins,
And tell me what is all this for?
To hope to find the Kingdom's door?

I long to see God's open space.
I long to see my mother's face.
My mind is filled with fear once more…
Will God give grace at Heaven's door?

35
THE CULT OF PERSONALITY

Demanding a crushing loyalty,
The Sublime is their reality,
Lifted up as though they are royalty,
The cult of personality.

Driven by 100 forms of fear,
Pay no mind to those below,
No one else seems quite so dear,
But, inside are dark and shallow.

They demand the final word,
Never knowing people`s reality,
Does this not strike a chord?
The cult of personality.

Tear me free of all confusion,
Stop this counter- revolution,
No more living an illusion,
We will have our restitution.

And then the talking heads will say,
We should never live this way,
Rebuild the former devastations
We now live in revelation.

Power will be from the people,

Our fathers knew the stark depravity,
 Let us gather at the steeple,
 No more cult of personality!

36
YOU WON, OR DID YOU?

I don`t have to be right anymore;
No longer a slave—addiction`s whore.
So tell me why you still want more?
There was only emptiness before.

Now then, let`s see—recount the past,
To those whose lives are always last,
They stalk and hunt a moment`s thrill;
Are they ever truly filled?

And in the end life has no more,
A lonely place—that's what`s in store.
You took all that you could not get,
It`s all destroyed with no regret.

But, have you really won yet still?
Does your life yet feel fulfilled?
Alone—that`s truly what you are;
And others watch you from afar.

37
ASHLEY SUE

A little girl with hair pure gold,
An uncle`s joy for him to hold.
I was there at your first step;
And also when the angels wept.

With dress and curls you'd step and smile;
The family`s joy for a little while.
You grew to be a beauty queen,
With goals to reach the silver screen.

But God, he had a different plan;
He never tells the mortal man.
His glory is for all to see,
Salvation is for all men free

And Ashley Sue would run her race,
She ran it at a young girls pace,
And in the end she was set free,
Salvations plan was hers to be.

I watched you fly away that night,
Loved ones prayed—eyes filled with fright.
The priest was down on bended knee,
But heaven called and set you free.

One day all men will fly away,
To be with God on that great day,

The Lord will keep you until then,
But I will see you once again!

38
THE WIND

Where do you come from my friend?
After you leave where do you end?
Sometimes I wish for your return,
Other times I am glad you are gone.

There are times when you are gentle;
Your movements, soft, cold, and calm.
Then…on the next occasion you`re brisk and strong.
Is there anyone who knows your secrets?

I wonder if they know where you have gone.
None who stand before you can win,
And the clouds? They need you to rain once again.
Oh, I wonder, can I give you my sin?

ABOUT THE AUTHOR

William Power is a freelance writer with an interest in poetry and short stories that explore life and the human heart. When he is not writing he enjoys being a father, a grandfather, and riding his vintage Harley Davidson in the North Georgia Mountains.

"I have always hoped to touch the lives of others through the written word. I thank each and every individual who has taken the time to read my poetry and prose. I write from the heart and touch on subjects that are not always pleasant, but, all of us have a level of neurosis I suppose, often times, these are the ties that bind us—I love to speak the language of the human heart."

William Power

Credits:

'The Kiss'

Francesco Hayez [Public domain], via Wikimedia Commons

Made in the USA
Charleston, SC
11 August 2012